Also by Tina D. Jones

Schoolmares

Max and Jeremy

By Tina D. Jones

Illustrated by Boris Radujko

For Franny, Steffen
+ Vincent.
Enjoy the story!
♥ Tina Jones

HMSI
Publishing L.L.C.
Plymouth, MI, U.S.A.
www.PublishHMSI.com

Max and Jeremy
First book of The Friends from Room 5

Published by HMSI Publishing L.L.C., a division of HMSI, inc.
www.PublishHMSI.com

Authored by Tina D. Jones
www.TinaDJones.com

Illustrated by Boris Radujko

Copy Editing by Monica Tombers, Patricia Berkopec
Cover Design by Elena Covalciuc
Interior Design by David R. Haslam

Publishing Coordinator: Jennelle Jones
Publisher: David R. Haslam

Producers: Lisa Merrill-Price and Robert Price

Published by HMSI Publishing L.L.C.

For information about permissions to reproduce any part of this work, write to
Permissions,
HMSI Publishing L.L.C.
Suite 3b,
50768 Van Buren Drive,
Plymouth, MI 48170, U.S.A.

ISBN – 10: 0-9842662-1-6
ISBN – 13: 978-0-9842662-1-0

Library of Congress Control Number: 2009940554

0047-0001

Printed in the United States of America

TKR 10 9 8 7 6 5 4 3 2 1
November 5th , 2009
19:01

In memory of my dad, Dan Drouillard, who believed in my writing before I did and from whom I learned the importance of a sense of humor and the ability to appreciate something in everyone.

Publishers Preface

It has been my honor to know and work with Tina for over ten years. I vividly remember, that day in May 1999, when my wife and I first walked into her classroom. We were assessing the multi-age program at Farrand Elementary School in Plymouth, Michigan. We had heard a lot about Tina from other members of the staff, along with comments from fellow parents who had been through the program with their children. We were very intrigued at what we would find.

Despite the first impression of chaos, after observing for a short time, we could see the level of respect and understanding in that classroom. The student-to-teacher relationship we had expected. But, the teacher-to-student and student-to-student aspects had to be seen to be believed! The tight, cooperative, integration between 3rd, 4th, and 5th Graders. Boys and girls sharing and helping each other (and at that age, the opposite sex ALWAYS has cooties...) and on top of that, students from different countries, including English as a second language children, and special needs students all took part seamlessly in the activities of the classroom. Our decision was made on the spot. Matt would become a member of the class the following school year.

Since then Tina and her family have remained friends with my family. Since then she has more than trebled her experience in teaching and, for want of a better word, classroom management. I am thrilled that Tina selected HMSI Publishing to produce and publish her first two books. *Max and Jeremy* is particularly exciting as the story shows how challenges can be overcome with the care and support of the adults involved in each child's education. I had multiple challenges to overcome during my education, but never came across a teacher like Tina to help me on my way. This is your chance to share part of her wisdom. I hope you enjoy reading it as much as we enjoyed producing it.

David R Haslam
Plymouth, Michigan
October 2009

Max and Jeremy

Chapter 1

"NO! Not *him!*" Jeremy's thought rang loudly in his head as he tried to understand what had happened. Just a few moments ago he had been excited about getting a partner for the state report project. Now Mrs. Reynolds had ruined it all. Instead of his best friend Habib, he was stuck with Max. Max! The kid who flapped his hands and spun in circles. The kid who chewed on his shirt all day long. The kid who didn't talk like the rest of them. Jeremy couldn't believe this turn of events.

During recess, Jeremy and Habib had been plotting how they could end up as partners for the project. They knew they'd make a great team. However, when they returned to class Mrs. Reynolds made the announcement that changed everything.

"OK, friends," she said, "I need you to make two even lines, one starting here behind Alex and the other starting behind Lily. You have one minute to find a place in either line. Ready? Go!" Jeremy rushed to stand next to Habib, who gave him a high five and a goofy grin.

"Time's up!" Mrs. Reynolds called loudly. The last few kids hurried into one line or the other. "Now I will give each of you a number between 1 and 13. Please remember your number. Lily 1, Habib 2, Paige 3, Jeremy 4..." The counting continued, but Jeremy had stopped listening. He didn't know what the numbers were for but thought it was a good sign that he and Habib both had even numbers. Then Mrs. Reynolds said the unexpected. "Your partner has the same number as you. When I call that number, come and get the study guide you'll need to begin your project. Remember that the first order of business is to pick the state you want to study. Ones, here you go..."

That's when Jeremy realized that Max was his partner. Disappointment made his stomach hurt. Without thinking, Jeremy rushed up to his teacher, tapped her arm and quietly begged, "Mrs. Reynolds, please give me a new partner. Anyone...just not Max, please!"

Mrs. Reynolds looked at him and said firmly, "I'm not switching anyone's partner, Jeremy. You haven't even started yet!" Max was still in the same spot, oblivious to what the other kids were doing. Mrs. Reynolds walked closer to Max and said "You'll be working with Jeremy, Max. Get your pencil and join him at the work table, OK?"

"OK, OK!" Max's voice was loud and he never looked at anyone when he spoke. "My pencil, my pencil!" he repeated as he half-ran back to his desk.

Jeremy knew that Mrs. Reynolds wouldn't give in. He grabbed the project packet and trudged over to the work table. Habib caught Jeremy's eye and made a face as he pointed at *Mental Max*, as the kids called him behind the teacher's back. Jeremy nodded once at him and flopped into his seat to wait for his new partner.

Chapter 2

Several minutes later, Max was still wandering around. Jeremy became more and more irritated as he watched him, sure that Max was trying to get out of doing any work. Jeremy found Mrs. Reynolds and complained. "Max isn't helping me! He hasn't even come to the table yet." Mrs. Reynolds nodded, saying "I noticed that Max didn't join you. I'll go get him." She walked over to Max and quietly spoke to him. She brought him to the table where Jeremy waited. "Here you go, Max!" Mrs. Reynolds said encouragingly. "Help Jeremy decide which state to study. You two have ten more minutes to figure that out."

Max sat down and began to rock and chew on his shirt. Jeremy stared at him although he knew it wasn't polite. He couldn't help it. Max was just so different. Max didn't seem to notice him at all.

After a few moments of silence Jeremy tried talking with him. "Do you know what state you want to study?" Max rocked faster in his seat, but he didn't answer or look at Jeremy. More silence followed while Jeremy waited for a response.

"Well, if you're not going to talk, then I'll decide for us. I want Florida." Jeremy watched Max for any sign that he had heard but Max was acting the same way. "Whatever," muttered Jeremy, getting up to go look through the books Mrs. Reynolds had brought in for the project.

Habib was at the book table when Jeremy got there. Leaning closer to him, Habib whispered "I can't believe you're stuck with *Mental Max*. That is just so wrong." Jeremy smiled a little at his best friend, glad at least *someone* understood what this meant to him. "I just can't believe this. Look at him over there. He's walking around flapping his hands like a bird. Want to trade partners?" Jeremy suggested with a hopeful look. Habib grimaced. "Ah, no thanks, I think I'm doing just fine with Rosalyn as my partner, even if she *is* a girl. Well, good luck. See ya later."

"Yeah, see ya," Jeremy replied glumly.

Jeremy spent a few more minutes selecting some interesting looking books about Florida and then headed back to the work table. He couldn't avoid this forever. Jeremy spotted Max still wandering around the room. Right then Jeremy decided to do the project without him. If he was going to get a good grade, he needed to just ignore Max and do it himself.

Chapter 3

Max came back to the table a while later and slammed down a toy dolphin he had taken from the reading nook. Jeremy looked up, startled at Max's sudden appearance. Max played with the dolphin, making squealing sounds that quickly drove Jeremy crazy.

"Would you stop that?" Jeremy barked. Max dropped the dolphin and practically ran back into the classroom. "Good riddance," Jeremy thought as he turned back to the study guide. "State facts," Jeremy read. "Hmmm...I have to find out about the area of the state, the population, and the date it became a state." Having some hard facts to research made Jeremy feel better about the whole thing. Facts were something he was really good at.

Jeremy opened up one of the books about Florida and quickly became lost in it. He loved the pictures of Daytona Beach and Cape Canaveral. Those were his favorite places to visit when he went to his Grandparent's house in Lakeland.

He took some notes and barely noticed when Max returned, this time holding a starfish he had found on the science shelf. Jeremy thought that maybe Max was trying to show it to him but he didn't care. He wanted nothing to do with Max.

Mrs. Reynolds called the class to the group area to check on the progress the partners had made with the project. Several pairs of kids raised their hands to share, telling about how they had already filled in two pages of the packet with facts. Mrs. Reynolds seemed really happy about how well everyone was doing. Jeremy was still upset with Mrs. Reynolds for sticking him with Max. He wasn't going to say anything unless he had to. Jeremy thought it unlikely that Max would choose to share. He hardly ever did.

Mrs. Reynolds seemed to sense Jeremy's uncooperative attitude because she didn't ask him to share. Instead, she told the class about the major parts of the project that they would need to complete by the following week.

"So after the packet is done, you and your partner will need to create a travel brochure to convince people to visit your state. It should have illustrations or photographs. We will complete the final drafts in the computer lab."

A murmur of excitement went through the class. Jeremy felt a spark of interest. He loved creating things in the computer lab. Even his mom and dad were amazed at how professional his work looked when he did it on the computer.

When Mrs. Reynolds mentioned the 3-D state map, Jeremy felt his heart race a little faster. He remembered his big brother Patrick's map from 5 years earlier. His brother had studied Michigan and had used real water for the Great Lakes. Although Jeremy wasn't very artistic, he'd find a way to make his Florida map look awesome.

As the students left the group area to get ready to go home, Jeremy felt his slowly growing bubble of anticipation burst. He had just spotted Max, still sitting on the carpet, rocking back and forth. How was he ever going to do a great project with *this* kid slowing him down? Jeremy's mood began to turn black again. He couldn't wait to get out of the classroom.

Chapter 4

At the end of the day Jeremy stomped over to his mom's car, flopped inside, and slammed the door shut.

"I'm glad to see you too!" his mom joked gently, trying to get a smile out of him. Jeremy glared out the window. His mom tried again. "So how was school?"

After a moment of silence, Jeremy burst out saying "Horrible! It was the worst day this year! We started our state projects and I got stuck with Max! He's so weird Mom. He chews on his shirt and it's so disgusting! I had to do everything and it's not fair!"

"He didn't help at all?"

"Not one bit, I swear it. Mrs. Reynolds didn't care either."

"Did you talk with her about it?"

"Yeah. I asked her for a new partner and she said no."

"Did she give you a reason?"

"No. It's just her rule about partners."

Finally, Jeremy's mom said, "Jeremy, I know how hard it can be to work with someone else. I have to do it at work all the time. Would you like to figure this out on your own or hear some ideas?"

Jeremy thought about this and then let out a frustrated sigh. "I guess I want ideas. I'm just upset because I've been looking forward to this project and now it's ruined." He paused, "at least I got to pick Florida!"

"Florida? Great! You're kind of an expert on that state, aren't you?"

Jeremy felt his mood lift a bit as he thought about his twice-yearly visits with his Grandparents in Florida. He had been all over that state and loved every minute of it. He was always trying to convince his parents to move there.

"Are you going to include information about The Daytona 500?" his mom asked.

"Duh!" Jeremy replied, but with a smile. He loved NASCAR racing and his dad and grandpa had taken him to a race last year. It had been the single most exciting event in his life. He even got Jeff Gordon's autograph!

"And I'm going to do a special part about the Kennedy Space Center. That was such a cool place."

"Do you still want to be an astronaut, like you did after we visited?"

"Mom!" Jeremy whined, "I was five when I wanted to do that. I want to race for NASCAR, remember?"

"Oh yeah, now I remember," she joked.

They talked about good times in Florida for a while, but then Jeremy's mom turned the conversation back to the problem with Max. Jeremy felt his enthusiasm fade.

"Did you still want my advice about your partner problem?" his mom asked.

"Yeah, I guess," Jeremy mumbled.

"Well, the first thing to remember is that no matter how strange Max seems to you, he's just a kid. Maybe he's just really shy. He might not be all that good at communicating, so he acts strangely."

"That's an understatement!" Jeremy complained.

His mom continued as though she hadn't heard the interruption. "Try to be patient and talk with Mrs. Reynolds again. She may have good advice. Then, if that doesn't work, try plan B."

"What's plan B?"

"I don't know yet, but there's always a plan B." She gave Jeremy a big smile and nudged him playfully. Jeremy rolled his eyes at her, but smiled too.

Chapter 5

The next morning Jeremy went into class a few minutes early. He wanted to talk with Mrs. Reynolds alone.

"Hi Jeremy!" Mrs. Reynolds called out with surprise when she noticed him. "You're here bright and early today."

"Uh, yeah," Jeremy began nervously, his words tumbling out in a rush. "I wanted to talk with you about the project. I want to do it by myself. I know I can get a good grade on it but not if Max is my partner. So can I?" Jeremy felt a little guilty asking about this after promising his mother he'd try working with Max. He just got so upset every time he thought about the project, and he didn't think he could survive another day of Max.

Mrs. Reynolds stopped putting mail into the students' cubbies and looked at Jeremy. "I think we already discussed this yesterday," she said, sounding disappointed.

"I know, and I tried to work with him, but I had to do everything. Everyone else has a partner that helps them and I have Max. It's not fair!"

Mrs. Reynolds was shaking her head no. "I'm sorry, Jeremy. I know Max wasn't much help to you yesterday but he *can* work on the project, in his own way." Jeremy heard himself blurt out "by walking around the room chewing on his shirt?"

Jeremy could tell that Mrs. Reynolds was trying to be patient with him. "Jeremy, Max *is* different from the other kids in this class. You're right about that. I can see how Max's behaviors upset you, but you need to understand that he isn't doing these things to get on your nerves. It's his way of calming down."

"How does *that* help him calm down?" Jeremy wondered out loud.

"Well, for Max, figuring out how to act around other people is like a big mystery. He doesn't know what to say or do. He finds it hard to talk to or even work with others. It's just how he is; it's not something he can help. I know it's hard, Jeremy, but those of us who find it easier to get along with others have to be patient and accept Max for who he is. He's a kid who wants the same things you do: to have fun and to have people be nice to him."

"That's kind of what my Mom said," Jeremy admitted.

"Smart Mom. Listen, when it comes time to work on the project I want you to talk with Max like you would anyone else. Read the questions to him and ask if he has any information. Sometimes Max can talk, especially when it's something he's excited about. We just have to find the ways Max can be involved. I can help you with that part."

Jeremy felt less upset. Then he remembered something. "You mean, like the time we were studying the life cycles of insects? He couldn't keep quiet. He knew everything about Monarch butterflies. *You* couldn't even get him to stop talking. That was funny."

Mrs. Reynolds nodded. "Exactly! Do you remember the life cycle he drew too?"

Jeremy did. It had been a great drawing, with labels and facts all over it. All of the kids had been impressed that Max could draw so well. Jeremy had completely forgotten about this until now. An idea came to Jeremy but he needed time to think. "Thanks for the help, Mrs. Reynolds. I think I'll give it another try."

"You're welcome, Jeremy!" Mrs. Reynolds replied as Jeremy went to the coat room to hang up his sweatshirt and backpack. Just then the morning bell rang.

Chapter 6

Later that day, Jeremy found Max already sitting at the work table. Max was racing a Matchbox car around, making loud engine noises as he moved it back and forth.

"Hi Max," Jeremy said, fighting the urge to say something rude. Max stopped the car but didn't say anything. Jeremy took a deep breath and made his best effort to sound friendly. "I brought over some books about Florida. Maybe we could look at the pictures and maps and see which places we want to include on the visitor's brochure, OK?"

Max grabbed a book and started looking through it. Mrs. Reynolds had reminded Jeremy that Max loved to read. The first page had a picture of a dolphin. Max yelled "Dolphin!" in excitement. He grabbed the toy dolphin from the table and showed it to the picture. He began making high-pitched dolphin screeches. Jeremy put his finger to his lips and said "Shhhhhh, Max. That hurts my ears. Please stop!"

"OK!" Max agreed loudly. He began reading the book instead.

Jeremy's attention turned to the Matchbox car again. Number 24? Jeff Gordon's car! "No way!" Jeremy yelled.

Jeremy's loud voice startled Max, causing him to cover his ears and jump up out of his seat.

"Do you like NASCAR, Max?"

Max smiled, grabbed the car and held it up in Jeremy's face. "Jeff Gordon, number 24. DuPont race car," he recited in a booming voice.

"I love Jeff Gordon. He's the best, isn't he?" Jeremy gushed with genuine excitement, surprised to discover that he and Max both liked the same driver. Jeremy realized that Max couldn't hear him because he was too busy rattling off every Jeff Gordon racing fact known to mankind. Jeremy almost laughed. It was so funny how once you got Max going on something, he was unstoppable. From what Jeremy could tell, he was also 100% right with his facts.

Almost as if someone had flipped on a light switch in a dark room, Jeremy began to see how Max could help him with the project. While he listened to Max ramble on about racing, the idea took shape.

"So Max," Jeremy interrupted, "Do you like play dough?"

Chapter 7

The next day Jeremy came into the classroom before the bell, more eager to work on the project than ever. He had asked Max to start the play dough map yesterday, just before he left for a dentist appointment. He couldn't wait to see how it was coming along.

He was blown away by what he saw at the work table. Max had created a nearly perfect shape of Florida with the play dough. There was a hole in the map for giant Lake Okefenokee and dark blue construction paper all around the edges for the ocean. What really surprised Jeremy was that Max had put the starfish right where Tampa Bay would be and the dolphin down by the city of Miami.

Jeremy ran to get Mrs. Reynolds, to show her Max's work. "He wasn't messing around at all, was he? He was trying to help all along."

Mrs. Reynolds looked at Jeremy and patted him on the shoulder. "I'm proud of you for figuring that out. Make sure you let Max know that you like his map, OK?"

"Like it? I *love* it!" Jeremy felt ready to burst. "Just wait until the other kids see it on presentation day! I need to find a way to hide it from the other kids until then. Do you have anything I can use?"

"Hmmm..." Mrs. Reynolds looked around the room. "Aha!" she exclaimed, walking toward the back cabinets. She grabbed a chair, stood on it and snagged a box from the top of the cabinets. She took off the lid and handed it to Jeremy, saying "That should do nicely."

"Let me see if it fits." Jeremy took the lid over to the Florida map and it settled over the map perfectly, hiding it from view. "Now it will be a surprise," Jeremy said with satisfaction. Jeremy realized that he was actually looking forward to seeing Max today. He wanted to talk about the map, but he also wanted to see if he could get Max to discuss the NASCAR race that had been on ESPN the night before. Habib hated racing and never listened when Jeremy went on and on about the details of the races he watched. Last night's had been *a real nail-biter*, as his dad liked to say. Jeff Gordon had won, but just barely. He figured if anything could get Max to talk to him, it would be the race.

A few short days ago, Jeremy would have never believed that he would seek out Max for a friendly chat. Another of his dad's favorite phrases came to mind. "Wonders never cease." That was dad's favorite thing to say when his brother Patrick announced that he was done with his homework early, without someone having to force him to do it. Jeremy thought it applied to this situation as well. He was actually starting to like Max!

Chapter 8

The big day finally arrived. Jeremy couldn't wait for the afternoon when his mom and all of the other parents would arrive to tour their "State Museum." This morning, however, was practice. He and Max were about to show off their presentation to their classmates. When Jeremy gave Max the signal, Max called out loudly, "Florida is the Sunshine State! Florida is the Sunshine State!"

Some of the kids giggled, including Habib, but Jeremy didn't care. He flashed a smile at the audience and announced "That's right, Max, and we're here to bring all of you a little bit of that sunshine! Here we go!"

Jeremy told the class all about Florida, as Max pointed out the places on their travel brochure and their display. Mrs. Reynolds had helped the boys work out a signal system to help Max know what to do during the presentation.

Finally, it was time to show the play dough map. Jeremy could hardly contain his excitement. "And now friends, let us introduce you to the amazing 3-D map of Florida!" Max lifted the box top off the map and the students immediately began to ooh and ah. Jeremy heard some kids saying "That's cool!" and "Wow!"

Jeremy drew their attention to every last detail. "This is Jeff Gordon's race car. It shows where Daytona Beach, home of the Daytona 500, is. Mickey Mouse is in Disney World, of course. The space shuttle is at the Kennedy Space Center."

The presentation was over more quickly than Jeremy could believe. He knew they were going to get a really good grade. "Are there any comments or questions?" he asked the audience.

After a burst of applause, nearly every hand went up. Jeremy called on Habib. "I liked your project, especially the cool map."

Kids nodded in agreement. Jeremy pointed to Max. "Here's the guy who made the map. Max did it all by himself. Didn't you, Buddy?"

Max began to spin around in excitement, calling out "Yep, yep," over and over. The class became quiet, except for a few giggles. No one seemed to know what to say. "Max also did the drawings for our project," Jeremy continued. "Aren't they great? Max is a good artist."

The kids crowded around the project to get a better look at the map and pictures. Some of the kids said "nice job, Max," as they went by him. Max moved away from the crowd looking for a quieter place to stand.

Jeremy followed him and said, "Max, I just wanted to say that I'm glad we were partners. I was lucky to have such a good artist on my team. Thanks Buddy."

He looked back at the group and saw Mrs. Reynolds looking at them. She gave him thumbs up. Jeremy grinned back, feeling happy and proud. He thought to himself that *this* was the beginning of a unique friendship!

Acknowledgements

First of all, I thank Marian for helping to nurture and shape the idea for this story. This story wouldn't exist without your influence.

Thanks to the many friends and colleagues who read it and gave their input, especially Susan, Kristi, and Debbie.

My thanks once again to Lisa and Bob, my supporters in more ways than one!

To David and Cecilia, thanks for your dedication, hard work, and belief in miracles.

I'm grateful to Boris for his talented depictions of these figments of my imagination, and his willingness to work with me to align things with my vision.

Thanks again to Elena, Jennelle (Ishi too!), Monica, and Pat for their work on this project and their attention to detail! I appreciate your levels of professionalism.

Thanks as well to my sisters, Donna and Linda, and to my mom, Barb, for their input, encouragement, and enthusiasm.

Thanks to my niece, Julie, for taking the pictures and making her aunt look good!

My eternal gratitude to my husband and children, who make this all possible. Go Team Jones!

Tina D. Jones
Ann Arbor, MI
October 2009

LaVergne, TN USA
17 November 2009
164309LV00002B/1/P

9 780984 266210